Published in 2015 by Plaister Press
10 9 8 7 6 5 4 3 2 1

British Library Cataloguing in Publication Data.
A catalogue record for this book is available from
the British Library.

Design: Lisa Kirkham

Printed in Poland

Plaister Press Ltd
Registered address:
3 King Street
Castle Hedingham
Halstead
Essex CO9 3ER
UK
www.plaisterpress.com

Mouse in the House

Gillian McClure

plaisterpress

They say there's a mouse *that* lives in this house.

Who's SEEN the mouse?

'I have,' says the bird
in the sky,

'from up above,
as I fly by.'

'I've seen the mouse
with my beady, bright eye.'

'I have,' says the squirrel in the tree,

'down the chimney, loud and clear.'

'I've heard the mouse
with my pricked-up ear.'

Who's SMELLED the mouse?

'I have,' says the dog
in the yard,

'close to the house
when the wind blows.'

'I've smelled the mouse
with my wet, black nose.'

Who's TOUCHED
the mouse?

'I have,' says the cat
at the door,
'just inside as it lay
on the floor.'

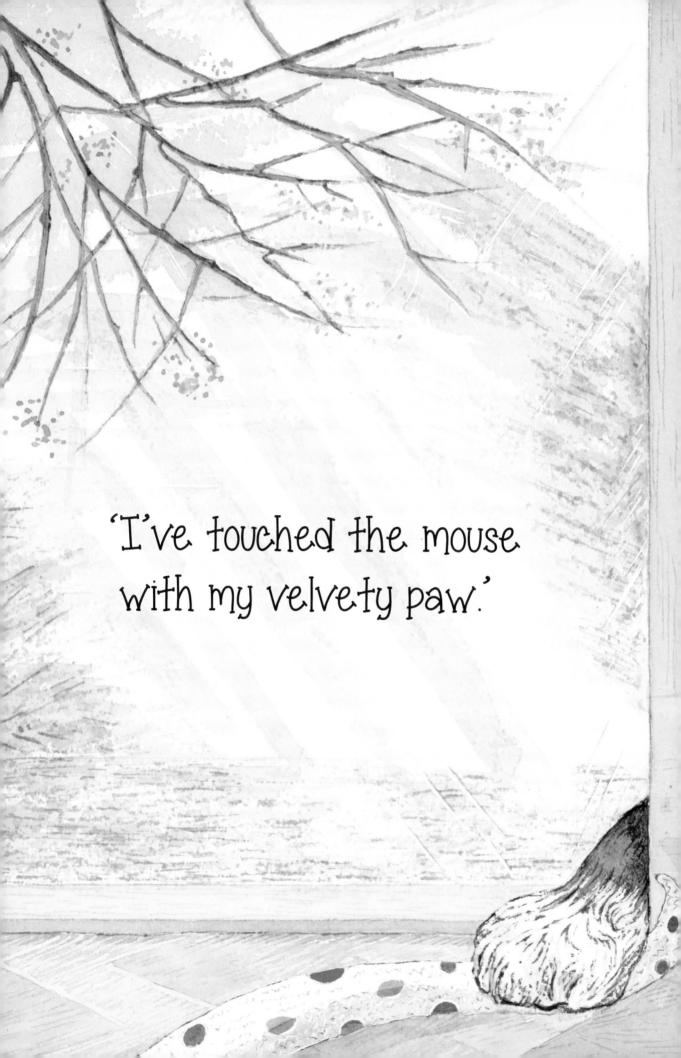

'I've touched the mouse
with my velvety paw.'

Who IS the mouse
that lives in this house?

It's a soft, toy mouse
with a squeak in its tail.

And who LOVES the mouse?

A baby loves
the mouse with
the squeak in
its tail,

and holds the mouse tight,
all through the night.

Sleep sweetly,
sleep soundly,
baby and mouse.

Connor lives in a house on a hill, with a garden where there is a squirrel in a tree and, high overhead, a hawk in the sky.

Other books by Gillian McClure from Plaister Press:
Selkie ISBN: 978-0-9565-108-0-8
The Little White Sprite ISBN: 978-0-9565-108-1-5
Zoe's Boat ISBN: 978-0-9565-108-2-2
We're Going to Build a Dam ISBN: 978-0-9565-108-4-6
Flood ISBN: 978-0-9565-108-5-3